XTREME SNAKES

PYTHONS

BY S.L. HAMILTON

A&D Xtreme
An imprint of Abdo Publishing | abdopublishing.com

abdopublishing.com

Published by Abdo Publishing, a division of ABDO, PO Box 398166, Minneapolis, Minnesota 55439.

Printed in the United States of America, North Mankato, MN.
032018
092018

THIS BOOK CONTAINS RECYCLED MATERIALS

Editor: John Hamilton
Copy Editor: Bridget O'Brien
Graphic Design: Sue Hamilton
Cover Design: Candice Keimig and Pakou Moua
Cover Photo: iStock
Interior Photos & Illustrations: Alamy-pg 32; Galileo Ramos-pgs 6-7; Minden Pictures-pgs 8-9, 10-11, 14-15 & 30-31; Science Source-pgs 16-17, 18-19 & 22-23; Shutterstock-pgs 1, 2-3, 4-5, 7, 12-13, 20-21, 26-27, 28 & 29 (bottom); Smithsonian Institution-pg 29 (top); USGS/Mike Rochford-pgs 24-25.

Library of Congress Control Number: 2017963891
Publisher's Cataloging-in-Publication Data
Names: Hamilton, S.L., author.
Title: Pythons / by S.L. Hamilton.
Description: Minneapolis, Minnesota : Abdo Publishing, 2019. | Series: Xtreme snakes | Includes online resources and index.
Identifiers: ISBN 9781532116032 (lib.bdg.) | ISBN 9781532156960 (ebook)
Subjects: LCSH: Pythons--Juvenile literature. | Constrictors (Snakes)--Juvenile literature. | Snakes--Juvenile literature. | Reptiles--Juvenile literature. | Herpetology--Juvenile literature.
Classification: DDC 597.967--dc23

CONTENTS

Pythons

Pythons are big, powerful snakes with muscular coils and a mouth full of sharp, backward-facing teeth. It is nearly impossible for their prey to escape once captured. The constrictor will hold tight with its teeth and its coils. Its victims cannot breathe, and soon the python has its meal.

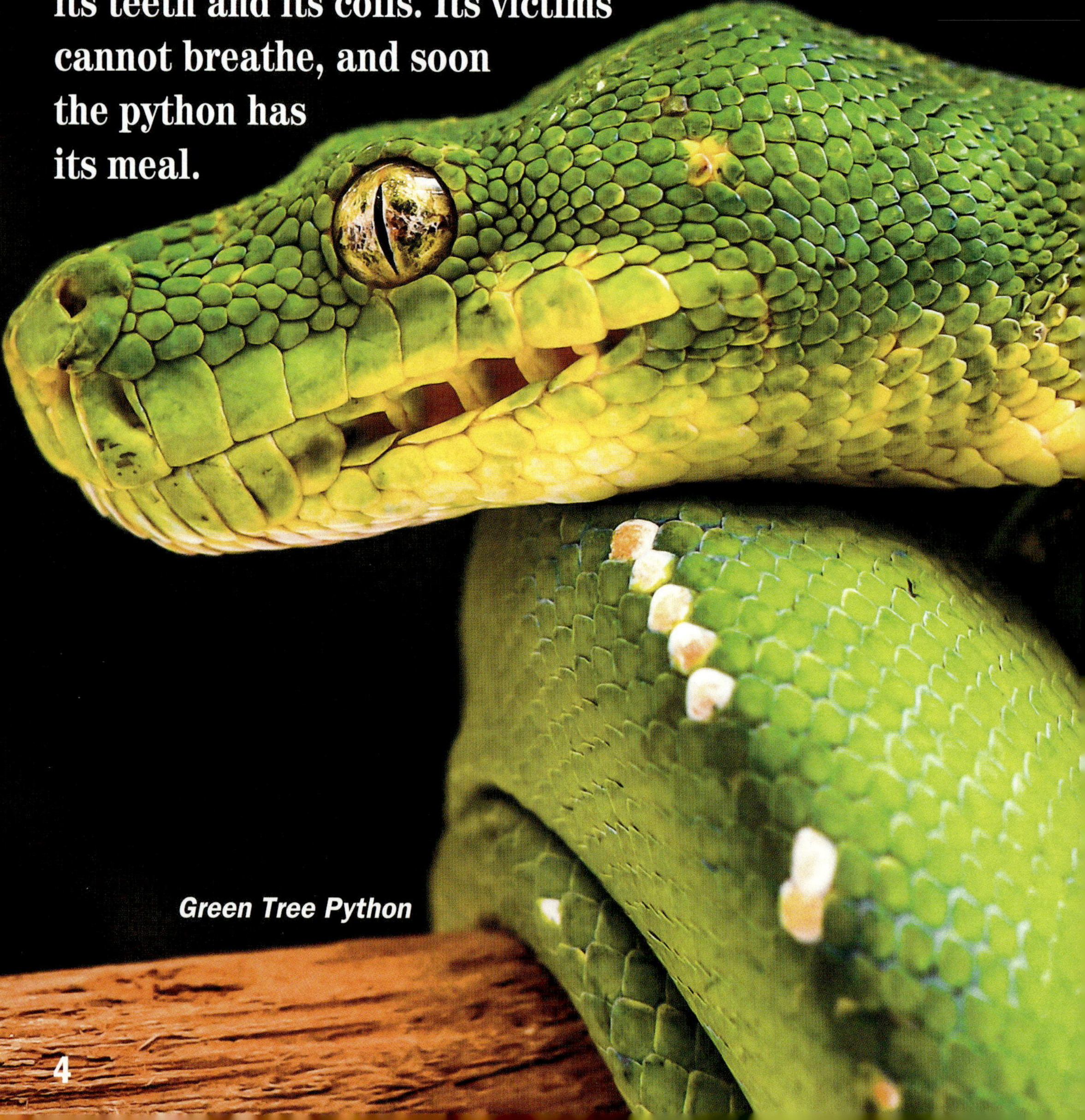

Green Tree Python

XTREME QUOTE – *"I've been bitten in the face by a python before and you don't want to experience that. It's like razor blades hitting you full in the face. You bleed... It's not fun at all."*

–Austin Stevens, Herpetologist

BODY PARTS

"Python" comes from the Greek word for the snake, *Pythonidae*. There are 41 species of pythons.

The jaw is divided into four independent parts. Each section is attached to the skull by super-flexible tendons and ligaments.

Sharp, backward-facing teeth.

XTREME FACT – A python can eat prey up to three times wider than its mouth.

Strong muscles move whole prey through the stomach. A python's stomach acid is so strong it can even dissolve bone. But the snake's digestion is very slow. If it swallows something big, it may only eat once per year.

Pythons can "see" prey using heat-seeking sensors called pit organs. Some pythons also have labial pits around their mouths that further aid them in finding prey.

Prey and Hunting

Pythons wait patiently for their prey. Their pit organs "see" the warmth given off by small- and medium-sized mammals, birds, and reptiles. The snakes' camouflage coloring makes them nearly invisible. When the victim comes close, the python strikes, capturing the animal with its teeth and then wrapping its coils around the prey's body.

An African rock python eats a Thomson's gazelle in Kenya, Africa.

Pythons constrict around the prey. When the animal breathes out, the python tightens more. It only takes a few minutes before blood can't get to the brain, the animal can no longer breathe, and it dies. A python eats the prey whole, starting from the head.

XTREME QUOTE* – *"The python glides over its meal like a sock over a leg." **–National Geographic Wild**

HABITAT

There are 41 species of pythons. They are native to Africa, Asia, and Australia. Pythons are found in rain forests, savannas, and deserts. They usually live near water. They are excellent swimmers. Pythons often wait for their prey to come for a drink and then attack, coiling themselves around their victim.

A reticulated python is coiled around a branch overlooking a stream in Borneo.

NESTING

A python mother makes a nest of leaves and dirt on the ground. Sometimes she will use another animal's burrow. The python mother lays 35 to 100 eggs. She circles herself around the eggs to keep them warm. If the temperature drops below 90 degrees Fahrenheit (32° C), the mother will shiver to create heat. She will guard the nest for up to 2 months. She does not eat this entire time and may lose up to half her body weight. Once the eggs begin to hatch, the mother leaves.

XTREME FACT – **Baby pythons are good hunters from the moment they hatch. However, hatchling pythons are also food for cobras, crocodiles, eagles, and large cats such as lions, tigers, and pumas.**

LARGEST PYTHONS

The reticulated python is the longest snake in the world. It makes its home in Southeast Asia. Reticulated pythons reach a length of 30 feet (9 m). They typically weigh about 250 pounds (113 kg), but the largest python grew to a huge 350 pounds (159 kg)! Only the green anaconda weighs more.

***XTREME FACT* – The reticulated python's name means "net-like" in Latin. It is named this because of the detailed pattern of its skin. The leather-like skin is used to make all types of clothing, shoes, and boots.**

People hold a 20-foot (6-m) -long reticulated python in Indonesia.

Smallest Pythons

The smallest pythons are anthill pythons. They are also called pygmy pythons. They grow to a length of only 20 inches (51 cm). These small pythons are found in western Australia. Temperatures there often reach 100 degrees Fahrenheit (38° C). To maintain a more even temperature, anthill pythons live in the cooler parts of termite mounds. They eat geckos, skinks, mice, and rats.

An anthill python eats a mouse.

XTREME FACT – Pythons often hunt and eat after pooping.

Thick Pythons

Blood pythons have short tails and thick bodies. Their shape makes them look overweight. Adults can weigh 40 to 45 pounds (18 to 20 kg), but their length is only about 4.5 to 6.5 feet (1 to 2 m). They are found in Malaysia, Sumatra, and Borneo. They bury themselves in leaf litter and blend in with their surroundings. This allows them to ambush their prey of rats, small mammals, and birds. They have heat-sensing pit organs on their upturned nose.

Blood pythons are so named because their backs can look blood-red in color.

XTREME FACT – Blood pythons can change the color of their heads. It is usually gray, but may change to black or red at different times of the day.

BEST DEFENSE

When threatened, ball pythons roll into a tight circle with their heads protected. This makes it difficult for predators, such as lions, leopards, warthogs, eagles, hawks, and cobras, to eat them. Ball pythons live in the dry grasses of Africa. They grow to a length of 5 feet (1.5 m).

XTREME FACT – Ball pythons are also known as royal pythons. They got this name because some African rulers wore these smaller-sized, gentle pythons as jewelry. Today, their calm nature makes ball pythons the most common pet pythons.

Climbing Pythons

A green tree python is a fast and safe climber. The snake uses a force called "concertina locomotion." It holds the vertical surface with a section of its coils in a super-strong grip. It then inches its head and front section upwards. The python continues to grip the tree and move itself up, section by section.

A juvenile New Guinea green tree python moves up a branch using concertina locomotion. Green tree pythons are born yellow, red, or brown in color. Most change to green as they get older.

Snake Handlers

Most humans try to stay away from wild pythons. Although pythons do not think of humans as food, the largest pythons can kill a person. But some people handle pythons in their work. Herpetologists go to college to learn about reptiles and amphibians. They work for zoos and museums, as well as companies that do research and environmental studies.

Wildlife removal experts are trained to capture and take away dangerous pests. Florida has a serious problem with Burmese pythons. Once exotic pets brought to the United States, these snakes grew too big. Owners illegally released them into nature. This invasive species eats the food of native predators, unbalancing the ecosystem. The state pays hunters to get pythons out of the Everglades.

University of Florida researchers capture a 15-foot (4.6-m) -long Burmese python weighing 162 pounds (73 kg). A 6-foot (2-m) -long American alligator was found in the snake's stomach.

If You Are Attacked

Python attacks are rare. They only attack humans if threatened or if they are starving. However, if you find yourself in the coils of a python, survival depends on trying these defenses:

1) Call for help IMMEDIATELY. Most survivors have had the help of other people. If the python bites you, you'll begin to lose blood. If the muscular coils wrap around your body, your heart will stop beating within minutes. Get help fast.

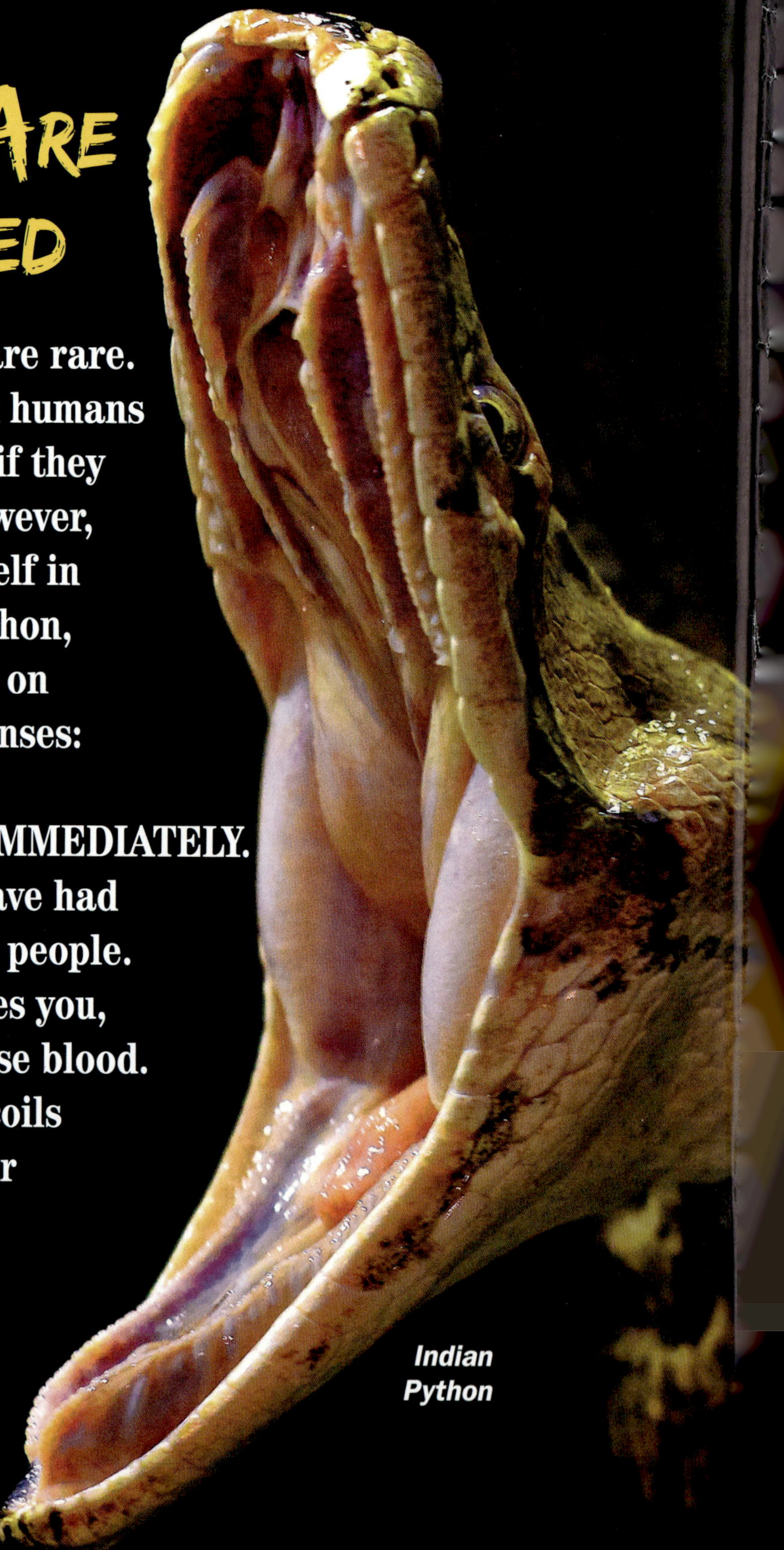

Indian Python

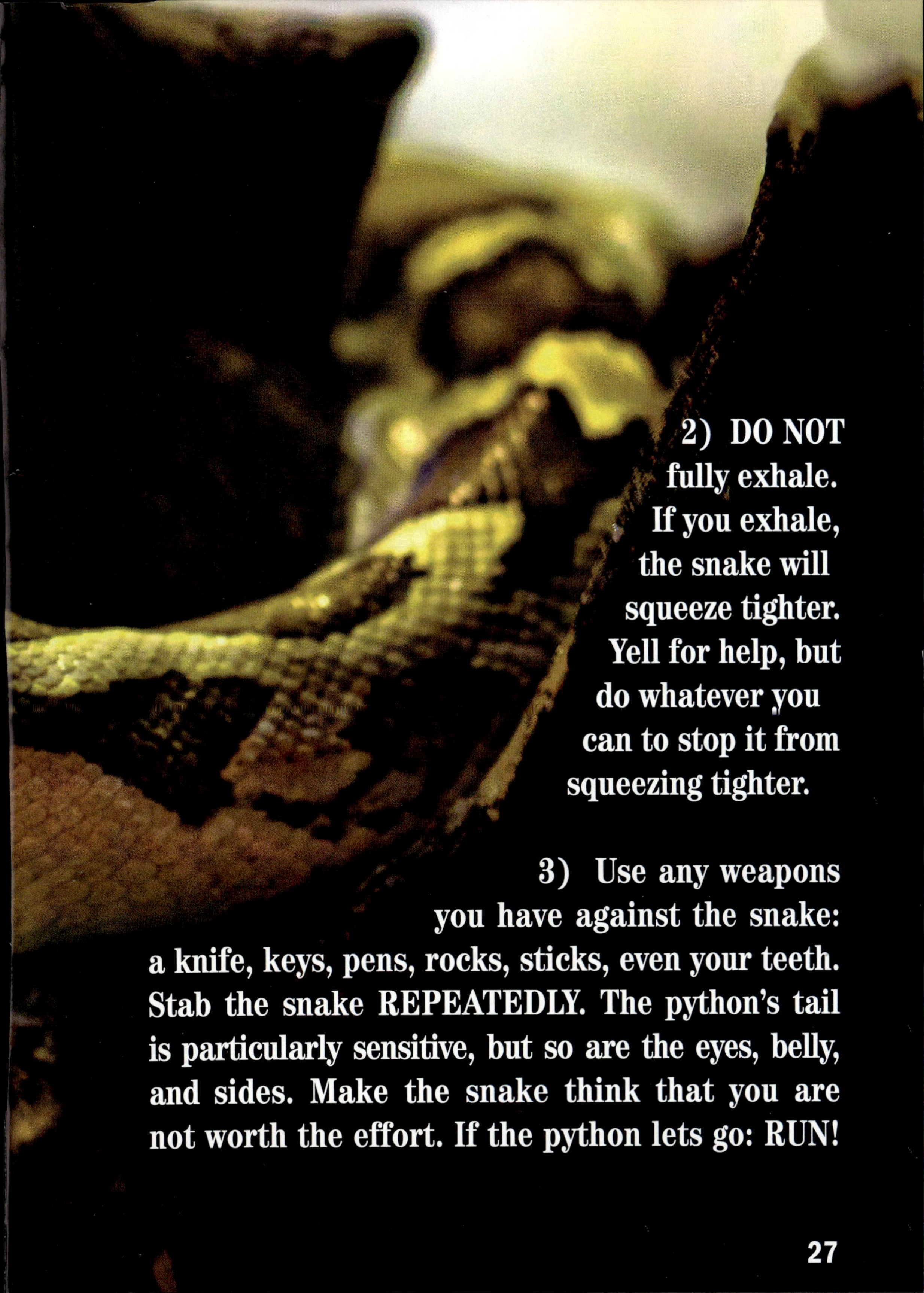

2) DO NOT fully exhale. If you exhale, the snake will squeeze tighter. Yell for help, but do whatever you can to stop it from squeezing tighter.

3) Use any weapons you have against the snake: a knife, keys, pens, rocks, sticks, even your teeth. Stab the snake REPEATEDLY. The python's tail is particularly sensitive, but so are the eyes, belly, and sides. Make the snake think that you are not worth the effort. If the python lets go: RUN!

Are They Endangered?

Most pythons are listed as "least concern" on the IUCN (International Union for Conservation of Nature) species list. However, Ramsay's python is listed as "endangered." The Myanmar short-tailed python and the Burmese python are listed as "vulnerable." They are hunted for food, clothing, and medicine. They are also captured as exotic pets. This, plus the loss of their habitat, puts these pythons at risk in their homelands.

Ramsay's Python

Myanmar Short-Tailed Python

Pythons help maintain a balanced ecosystem in their native homes. Humans need to be aware of these dangerous, but beautiful, snakes as they share their world with them.

Burmese Python

GLOSSARY

AMBUSH
A surprise attack by something hiding nearby.

CAMOUFLAGE
Coloring and/or physical appearance that allows a creature to blend in with its surroundings.

ECOSYSTEM
A biological community of animals, plants, and bacteria that live together in the same physical or chemical environment.

ENDANGERED
When there are so few numbers of a plant or animal, it is close to becoming extinct.

EXOTIC PETS
Unusual or rare pets that often come from another country. Sometimes exotic pets are illegal to own. Some python species are considered an exotic pet.

INVASIVE SPECIES
A plant or animal not normally found in an ecosystem; often introduced accidentally. Invasive species with no natural predators can greatly harm native plants and animals.

Black-Headed Python

Savanna
An area of grassland with few trees.

Species
A group of plants or animals that are related to one another. They look alike and may produce offspring.

Vulnerable
When a plant or animal is at risk of becoming "endangered" unless changes are made to its situation.

Online Resources

Booklinks
NONFICTION NETWORK
FREE! ONLINE NONFICTION RESOURCES

To learn more about pythons, visit abdobooklinks.com. These links are routinely monitored and updated to provide the most current information available.

INDEX